Sinbad
the Sailor

A Parragon Book

Published by
Parragon Books,
Unit 13–17, Avonbridge Trading Estate,
Atlantic Road, Avonmouth, Bristol BS11 9QD

Produced by
The Templar Company plc,
Pippbrook Mill, London Road, Dorking, Surrey RH4 1JE

Designed by Mark Kingsley-Monks

Printed and bound in Italy

ISBN 0-75250-914-4

Sinbad
the Sailor

Retold by Caroline Repchuk
Illustrated by Helen Cockburn

||| •PARRAGON• |||

This is the story of Sinbad the Sailor and some of his strange adventures at sea. He travelled far and wide and each voyage brought danger and excitement.

His first voyage was on a ship bound for the east Indies. One day it stopped at a strange little island, which was smooth and green.

The crew had just set up camp when the island began to shake. It was not an island at all, but the back of a whale!

The sailors rushed back to the ship, but Sinbad was left behind. He clung to a piece of driftwood, and next day was washed up on an island.

Sinbad set out to explore the island, and found a huge white egg. It belonged to a gigantic bird called a Roc. Sinbad was eager to leave the island, so he tied himself to the Roc's foot while it slept, and the next day it carried him to a rocky valley surrounded by mountains.

The valley floor was covered with diamonds, but they were guarded by fierce giant serpents. Sinbad hid in a tiny cave, where the serpents could not reach him.

He had heard of the Valley of Diamonds, and knew some men had found a way to reach the gems.

They threw meat into the valley, which huge eagles carried back to their nests. Then they scared them off, and gathered the diamonds which had stuck to the meat.

After filling his pockets with jewels Sinbad tied himself to a piece of meat, which was seized by a huge eagle and carried out of the valley.

The diamond hunter was shocked when Sinbad dropped into the nest, but soon helped him when Sinbad showed him his pockets full of gems.

After a few months at home, Sinbad longed for adventure again, so he set sail on a merchant ship. But a violent storm blew up, driving them towards the Island of the Ape Men.

The fearsome Ape Men stormed the ship, forcing the crew to swim ashore.

There they found a magnificent palace, which belonged to a terrifying ogre. Soon they were captured, and the ogre began to eat them one by one! Quickly they made a plan for escape.

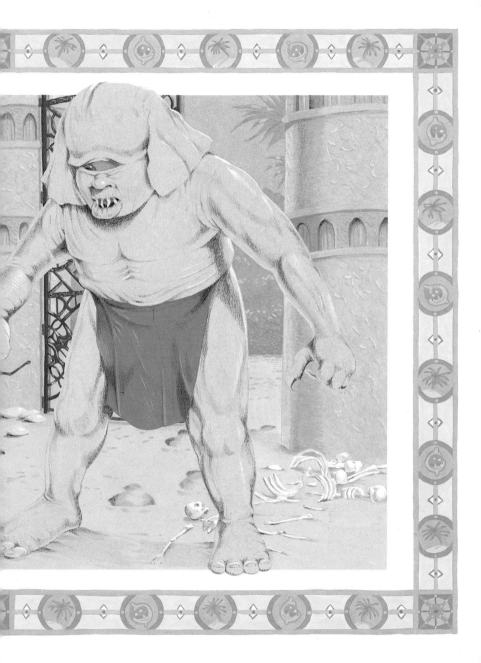

They made wooden rafts which they carefully hid, then as the ogre slept they thrust a red hot poker into his one great eye, hoping to kill him.

But with a howl he staggered to his feet. The men lost their nerve, and ran to the beach with their rafts, rushing into the sea as fast as they could.

The ogre and his hideous wife followed, and threw huge boulders at them, sinking most of the rafts. Soon only Sinbad and two others were left alive. They were tossed around in the stormy sea, but at last washed up on another island.

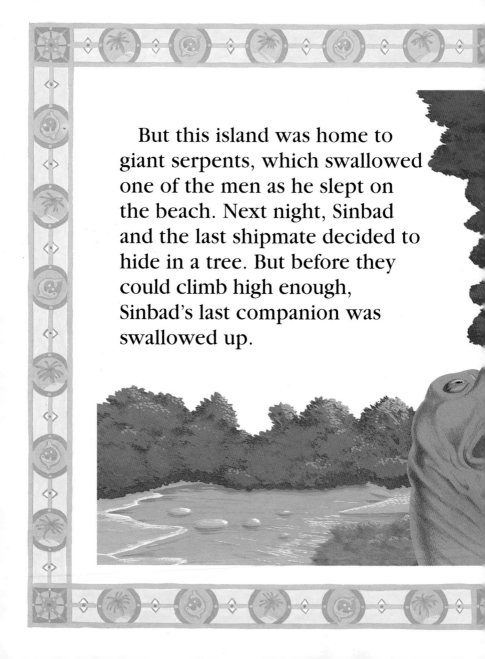

But this island was home to giant serpents, which swallowed one of the men as he slept on the beach. Next night, Sinbad and the last shipmate decided to hide in a tree. But before they could climb high enough, Sinbad's last companion was swallowed up.

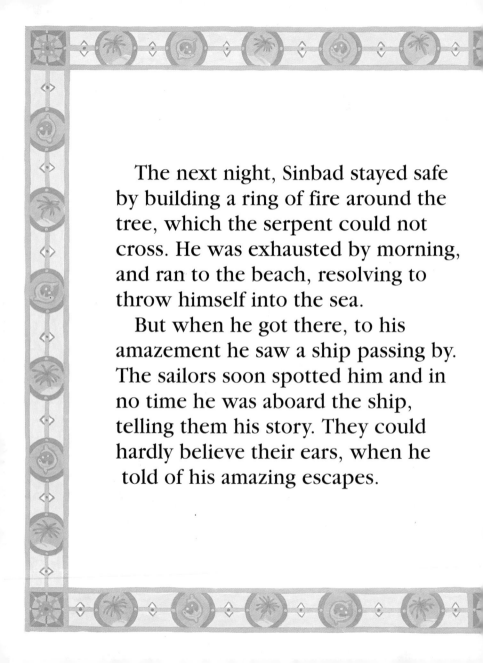

The next night, Sinbad stayed safe by building a ring of fire around the tree, which the serpent could not cross. He was exhausted by morning, and ran to the beach, resolving to throw himself into the sea.

But when he got there, to his amazement he saw a ship passing by. The sailors soon spotted him and in no time he was aboard the ship, telling them his story. They could hardly believe their ears, when he told of his amazing escapes.

As they sailed home they saw many wonders, such as a giant sea tortoise. Sinbad's family were delighted to see him, but after a few months he eagerly set sail again.

After a long voyage, the ship arrived at an island. The crew were starving, and foolishly cooked a young Roc bird, just hatched from its egg. Its gigantic parents were frantic when they returned to the nest and found that it was empty.

The men ran for the ship, but there was no escape. The Roc birds were furious, and headed after the ship clutching huge boulders in their talons.

With careful aim they dropped the boulders on the middle of the ship and it broke into a thousand pieces. Every man on board was thrown into the sea.

Once again Sinbad found himself clinging to a piece of driftwood. One by one his shipmates drowned, until only he was left. At last he washed up on a sandy shore.

Gathering all his strength he set off to explore inland.

He had not gone far, when he saw a feeble old man sitting by a brook, who motioned to be carried across. Sinbad gladly took the man on his shoulders. But when he reached the other side, the man would not get down. He gripped Sinbad tightly with his legs and forced him to carry on.

The wicked man kept hold of him thus for a week, wearing him into the ground. In desperation, Sinbad made some wine with grapes he found, and the old man demanded to taste it. Soon he had drunk too much and fell from Sinbad's shoulders in a stupor.

Later Sinbad learnt he was the old man of the sea, and that no-one before had ever escaped him.

Sinbad headed straight for the shore, and was luckily picked up by a merchant ship, headed for an island renowned for its coconuts. They threw stones at the monkeys in the trees, and the furious monkeys grabbed the nearest missiles to hand — the coconuts! Soon they returned to the ship with plenty of coconuts to trade at the next port.

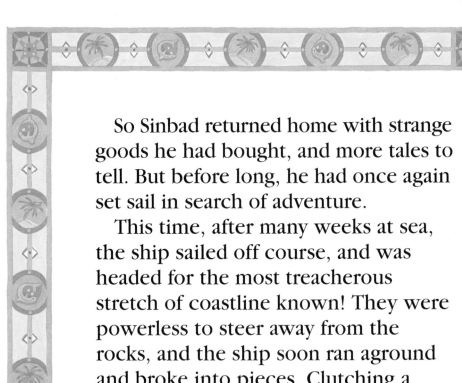

So Sinbad returned home with strange goods he had bought, and more tales to tell. But before long, he had once again set sail in search of adventure.

This time, after many weeks at sea, the ship sailed off course, and was headed for the most treacherous stretch of coastline known! They were powerless to steer away from the rocks, and the ship soon ran aground and broke into pieces. Clutching a small raft, Sinbad was swept into a channel, which ran inland and disappeared underground. When he came once more into daylight he was captured by natives who took him to their King.

Sinbad entertained the King with tales of his adventures, and presented him with gifts from the goods he had rescued on his raft.

The King was delighted, and sent Sinbad home with presents for his Sultan. Seated on his elephant, the King led a great procession to the harbour to wave farewell.

When Sinbad arrived home he hurried to the Sultan's palace. The Sultan was impressed by the generous gifts, and sent Sinbad to sail back at once with costly presents in return.

The King was delighted to receive Sinbad and his gifts, and a bond of friendship was declared between the two countries.

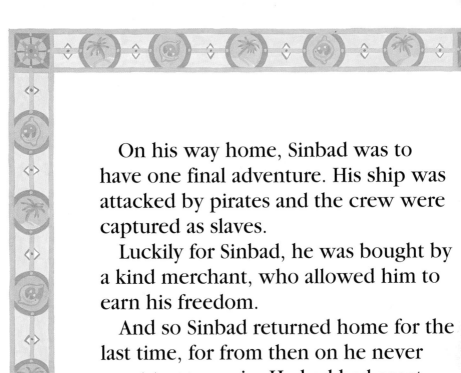

On his way home, Sinbad was to have one final adventure. His ship was attacked by pirates and the crew were captured as slaves.

Luckily for Sinbad, he was bought by a kind merchant, who allowed him to earn his freedom.

And so Sinbad returned home for the last time, for from then on he never went to sea again. He had had great adventures and escaped danger and death more times than he could remember. Now he wished to spend the rest of his life safely at home with his family and friends.

Sinbad the Sailor belongs to one of the greatest story collections of all time: *The Tales of the Arabian Nights*, also known as *The Book of One Thousand and One Nights*. These stories were first heard many hundreds of years ago and include *Aladdin and the Wonderful Lamp*, *Ali Baba and the Forty Thieves* and *The Magic Carpet*. The story goes that they were originally told by the beautiful Princess Scheherezade to the suspicious Prince of Tartary, who had threatened to behead her at daybreak. But her tales were so exciting that, as the sun rose, he longed to hear how they ended and so pardoned her life for one more day, until after one thousand and one nights Scheherezade had won his trust and his heart.

This
Treasure Cove Story
belongs to

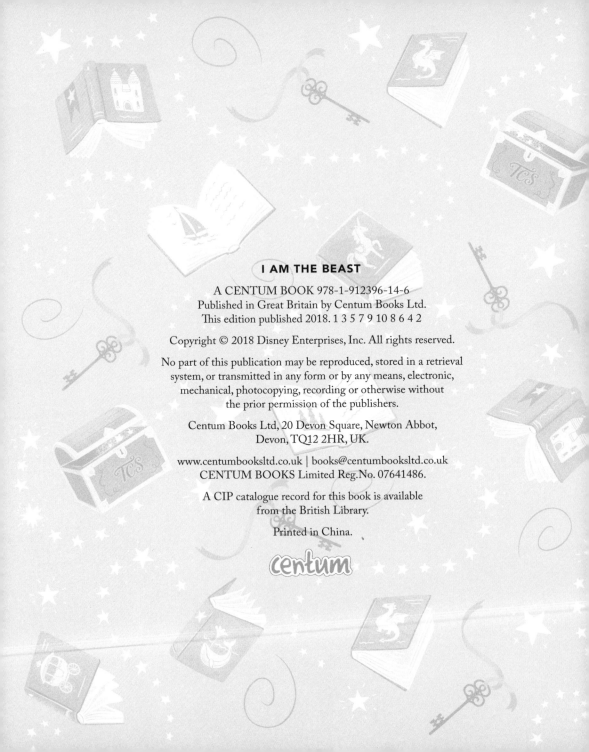

I AM THE BEAST

A CENTUM BOOK 978-1-912396-14-6
Published in Great Britain by Centum Books Ltd.
This edition published 2018. 1 3 5 7 9 10 8 6 4 2

Centum Books Ltd, 20 Devon Square, Newton Abbot,
Devon, TQ12 2HR, UK.

www.centumbooksltd.co.uk | books@centumbooksltd.co.uk
CENTUM BOOKS Limited Reg.No. 07641486.

A CIP catalogue record for this book is available
from the British Library.

Printed in China.

DISNEY
PRINCESS

Beauty and the Beast

I Am the Beast

By Andrea Posner-Sanchez
Illustrated by Alan Batson

I am the

BEAST.

I have horns, claws
and I'm covered in fur.

I live in a
huge
castle
deep in the woods.

I used to be
a human prince.
I had power and
riches, but I didn't
care about anyone
except myself.

I don't like roses.

An old beggar woman once asked permission to stay in my castle in exchange for a rose. I laughed at her and told her to leave.

The woman was an
enchantress in disguise!
As punishment for my lack
of kindness, she turned me
into a beast and put a curse
on all who lived in my castle.

My loyal servants were transformed
into enchanted household objects.

Lumiere became a candelabrum.

Cogsworth turned into a clock.

Mrs Potts became a teapot.

And her son, *Chip*, became a teacup.

The enchantress left a magical
rose in the West Wing of my castle.

If all the flower's
petals
fell

before I learned to love someone
– and won her love as well – we
would stay cursed forever.

I'm not a good host.

The first visitor to my castle in years was a man named *Maurice*. I locked him in my dungeon.

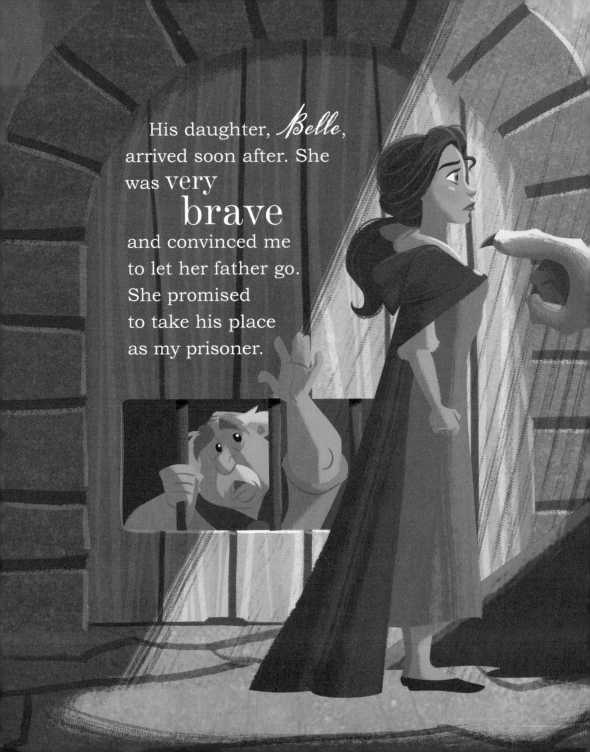

His daughter, *Belle*,
arrived soon after. She
was very
brave
and convinced me
to let her father go.
She promised
to take his place
as my prisoner.

I have a bit of a TEMPER. When I caught Belle trespassing in the West Wing, I was scared she was going to touch the rose.

I YELLED so loudly she ran right out of the castle.

I am **big** and **strong,**

but fighting off a pack
of wolves wasn't easy.

I can be
CRANKY
when I'm hurt. Belle was patient
as she cleaned my wounds.

Small animals used to be afraid
of me. Belle taught me how to be
gentle and kind.

You might think I have bad table manners…

...but it's hard to hold a spoon
with these giant, furry beast hands!

I don't look graceful. Turns out I'm a good dancer – with the right partner!

Falling in love with Belle was easy, but I never expected her to love me in return. She is a special person. She saw past my hideous exterior.

Thanks to Belle's love, the curse was lifted.

I am the Beast no more.

Treasure Cove Stories

Book list may be subject to change.

An ongoing series to collect and enjoy!